PETER RABBIT™
HEAD Over TAIL

For Mandy, a maker of dreams-come-true.
And for River and Sky, my two little clever rabbits x — RB

For my mum and dad, who introduced me
to Peter Rabbit when I was little — NK

PUFFIN BOOKS

UK | USA | Canada | Ireland | Australia
India | New Zealand | South Africa

Puffin Books is part of the Penguin Random House group of companies
whose addresses can be found at global.penguinrandomhouse.com.

www.penguin.co.uk   www.puffin.co.uk   www.ladybird.co.uk

Penguin
Random House
UK

First published 2021
001

Text and illustrations copyright © Frederick Warne & Co. Ltd, 2021
Text by Rachel Bright. Illustrations by Nicola Kinnear
Peter Rabbit™ & Beatrix Potter™ Frederick Warne & Co.
Frederick Warne & Co. is the owner of all rights, copyrights and
trademarks in the Beatrix Potter character names and illustrations

Printed in China

The authorized representative in the EEA is Penguin Random House Ireland,
Morrison Chambers, 32 Nassau Street, Dublin D02 YH68

A CIP catalogue record for this book is available from the British Library

ISBN: 978–0–241–43172–6

All correspondence to:
Puffin Books
Penguin Random House Children's
One Embassy Gardens, 8 Viaduct Gardens, London SW11 7BW

MIX
Paper from
responsible sources
FSC
www.fsc.org   FSC® C018179

PETER RABBIT™
HEAD OVER TAIL

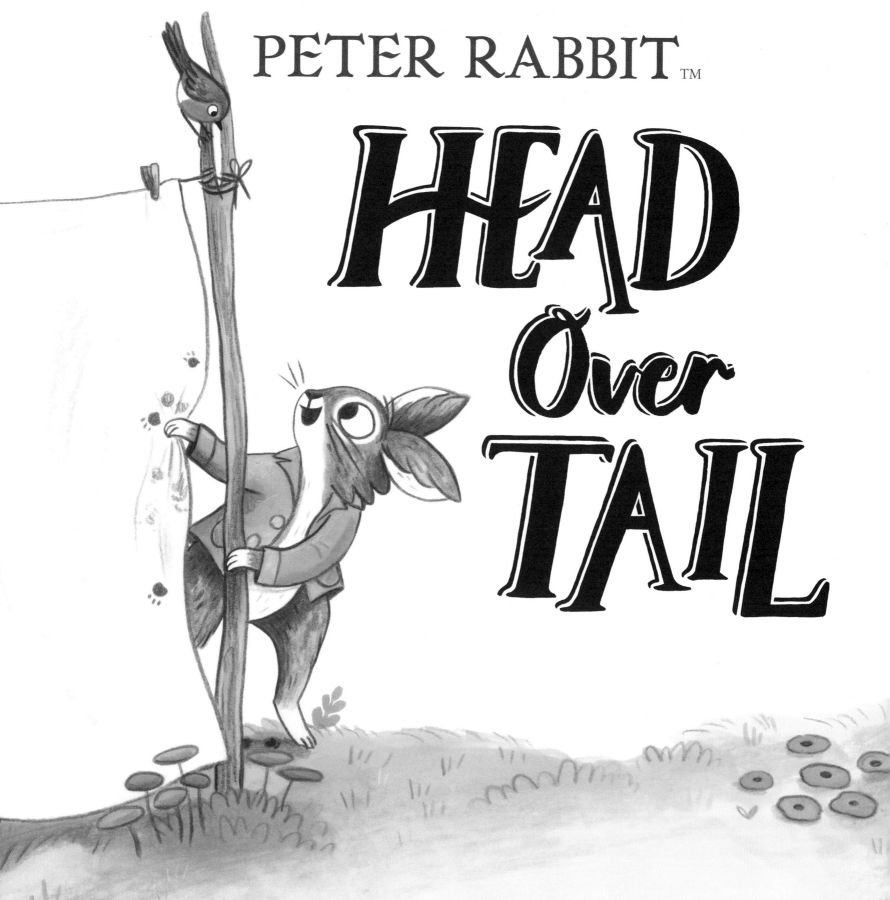

Rachel Bright Nicola Kinnear

PUFFIN

Once, beneath a hillside,
drenched in drips of summer rain,
lived a fellow, quite amazing,
with a very busy brain!

And if you look quite closely,
I think you'll see him too . . .
Two ears, some twitching whiskers
and a flash of something blue . . .

This is **PETER RABBIT!**

He is handsome, young and smart.

He's also rather clever,

which is where our story starts.

He was sketching in his bedroom,
in his big inventions book,
when a voice from in the kitchen
shouted, "Children? Oh dear . . ."

"... *LOOK!*"

Mama clutched the linens.
"Just look at all this sploshing!
There's muddy little paw prints
smudged **ALL OVER** my clean washing!"

Peter glanced (quite sheepishly)
upon his grubby paws,
and thought perhaps, *just maybe,*
HE might have been the cause . . .

"I'll help you!" answered Peter.

He knew **_exactly_** what to do!

Clutching at his book, he said,

"I'll make them good as new!"

He had thought of an invention!

In his eye, a little twinkle . . .

I'll make a 'magic' **WASHING LINE**

to Mrs Tiggy-Winkle!

She was a laundry **expert**,

who did everything precisely.

He was sure she'd do it for him

if he asked her very nicely.

She'd wash and press it in a flash,
much faster than he could.
And that would leave more time to play,
which in **HIS** book, was good!

My House

Rope

Ivy

Washing

Mrs Tiggy-Winkle's House

So, he called for Squirrel Nutkin,
who came running with a grin.
When he heard of Peter's plan,
he was **EXCITED** to join in!

Nutkin scampered quickly
across the forest floor,
to tie the line up tightly
near Mrs Tiggy-Winkle's door.

Then Peter looped some ivy
round the magic washing line
and waited for a signal that
would tell him it was time.

When Squirrel Nutkin tugged,
he'd go upon the count of three.
One and **TWO** and . . .

. . . Peter **LEAPED!**

And flew out of the tree.

He **ZOOMED** across the canopy
and gathered up some speed!
His latest master plan was working
VERY *well indeed!*

But when he reached the spot
where Squirrel Nutkin was now standing,
he realized then he hadn't thought
about a *nice* **SOFT LANDING!**

Mrs Tiggy-Winkle,
when she opened up her door,
was surprised to see a pile of sheets
and Peter on the floor!

She bundled up the washing
and ushered them inside,
into her cosy kitchen
with efficiency and pride.

And in two slices and two cups,
the laundry . . . it was done.
Soon Peter could get back
to being **WILD** and having fun!

He said a gracious "thank you"
and climbed up to the line,
as Squirrel Nutkin shouted out:
"*I* want to ride this time!"

But **TWO** was rather heavy
for a comfy journey back.
It was built for just one Peter . . .

. . . so the washing line went slack!

As they **ZIPPED** along the straining line,
they very quickly found
their bottoms getting closer
to the rising-upwards ground!

As problems go, this one came fast
and rapidly got **BIG**.
They **CRASHED** and **BASHED**
through leaves and flowers . . .

. . . and one *quite* **PAINFUL** twig.

A bouncing ball of tails and ears,
they rolled along the ground.
No sooner were they right-way-up,
they'd be back **UPSIDE-DOWNED!**

All bundled up and spinning fast,
it really was a muddle –
one that kept on rolling them
right through a muddy puddle!

They rolled and rolled until
they stopped at two familiar feet,
probably the **LAST** ones
Peter might have hoped to meet . . .

And slowly, as the sheets unfurled,
they showed a coloured mess . . .
Peter thought about how best
a rabbit should confess!

But before the words had crossed his lips,
his mama rabbit gasped!
Her eyes were huge, her mouth was wide,
her paws were tightly clasped!

"Oh! I *love* them, Peter Rabbit!
Brand-new sheets for all the beds!
Such pretty patterned colours,
where you all will lay your heads!"

And everyone praised Peter
for his very clever thinking,
as Squirrel Nutkin shook his head,
chuckling and winking . . .

But later on that evening,
Mama took him to one side,
to explain a job done **CAREFULLY**
would fill him up with pride.

Peter thought about her words
and stretched up on tiptoes,
to say a whispered "sorry"
with a kiss upon her nose.

Tomorrow was another day
who knew what it might bring?
Well, certainly a chance to build
an even **BETTER** thing!

Peter's Inventions

He'd dream of new inventions
he could scribble and create.
Practising is, after all,
what makes a rabbit great!

Good night then, Peter Rabbit,
we'll let you dream away,
and see you on the hillside
another wild, free day.